Down on the Farm

NAOMI

Down on

Rita Lascaro

Green Light Readers
Harcourt Brace & Company
San Diego   New York   London

First Green Light Readers edition 1999
Green Light Readers is a trademark of Harcourt Brace & Company.

Library of Congress Cataloging-in-Publication Data
Lascaro, Rita.
Down on the farm/Rita Lascaro.
p.   cm.
"Green Light Readers."
Summary: A child naps like the cat, flaps like the hen, swims like the duck,
and imitates the other animals on the farm.
ISBN 0-15-202000-4
[1. Domestic animals—Fiction.]   I. Title.
PZ7.L3265Do   1999
[E]—dc21   98-15567

A C E F D B

Printed in Hong Kong

I see my dog play.

I can play like my dog.

I see my cat nap.

I can nap like my cat.

I see my hen flap.

I can flap like my hen.

I see my duck swim.

I can swim like my duck.

I see my friends ride.

I can ride like my friends . . .

. . . down on the farm.

The illustrations in this book were done in colored pencil with collage
created from cut and torn handmade paper.
The display type was set in Futura and hand lettered by Rita Lascaro.
The text type was set in Minion.
Color separations by Bright Arts Ltd., Hong Kong
Printed by South China Printing Company, Ltd., Hong Kong
This book was printed on 140-gsm matte art paper.
Production supervision by Stanley Redfern and Ginger Boyer
Designed by Barry Age